For

MICHAEL

who could have stopped that ball

This edition is printed and distributed by special arrangement
with the originators and publishers of
BEGINNER BOOKS, Random House, Inc., New York, by
E. M. HALE AND COMPANY

STOP THAT BALL!

BY MIKE McCLINTOCK

ILLUSTRATED BY FRITZ SIEBEL

Beginner Books

A DIVISION OF RANDOM HOUSE, INC.

I hit my ball. I made it fly.

I hit my ball as it went by.

It went around and then came back.

I gave my ball another WHACK!

I hit it high.

I hit it low.

I hit so hard the string let go!

The string let go.

There went my ball.

Away up high,

Out past the wall!

So I ran fast around the wall.

I had to get my big red ball.

I saw it jump. I saw it roll,

And head right for an open hole.

The hole was deep. The hole was black.

How could I get my red ball back?

What could I do?

Say! This was bad!

This was the only ball I had.

And then a man put out his head.

"You hit me with your ball!" he said.

He was so mad he sent my ball

Way down the hill. I saw it fall.

I saw my red ball take a hop

And you know where I saw it stop!

I saw it hop right on a truck.

Oh, what a shame! Oh, what bad luck!

11

The truck went down the hill, and so,

I ran as fast as I could go.

"Look here!" I called.

I called out, "Say!

You must not take my ball away."

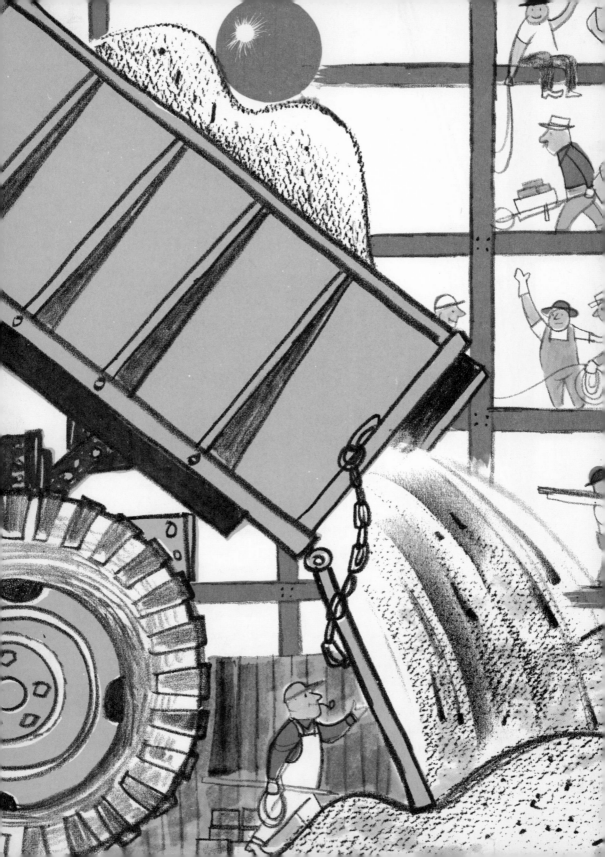

At last the truck came to a stop,

And my red ball was up on top.

I saw the truck back up to dump.

The sand came out.

I had to jump!

The sand came out.

So did my ball.

I saw it jump and bump a wall.

I saw it jump right in a box.

I saw it land up on some blocks.

And there it sat.

I said, "I bet

That ball will not

Be hard to get."

Oh! Oh! Now here was something new!

The box went up!

My ball went, too!

It went up high.

What should I do?

I just could not sit here and whine.

I had to get that ball of mine.

"Here is your ball," called out a man.

"Now run and get it if you can!"

And then he gave my ball a kick.

Oh what a trick! Oh what a trick!

Now, could I get it? I could try!

My dog ran fast and so did I.

But not a thing went right that day.

That dog of mine got in my way.

Then down I went, and so did he.

My ball went on ahead of me.

My big red ball went on its way.

Would things go on like this all day?

A man said, "Stop!

Stop! Keep away!

Do not go near that hill, I say!

We are about to blow it up,

So stop right here,

And hold your pup!"

There was my ball—my only ball.

I could not get it after all!

25

Then BOOM! BOOM! BOOM!

Oh, what a thump!

I saw the hill just kind of jump.

And then it shot up in the air,

And bits of it went here and there.

Where was my ball?

Where did it go?

I could not see it high or low.

Then, there it was! High as a kite!

Now I could get my ball all right.

I said, "I know it must come down.

And it will fall somewhere in town.

Then I can find it. Yes, I can!"

And so I ran and ran and ran.

I saw a house on fire ahead.

"My ball must not land there!" I said.

"For if it does, it's gone for ever!

And I will never get it! Never!"

But then some water
Shot up high.
It hit my ball
And made it fly.
Boy! Was I happy!
This was fine!
Now I could get
That ball of mine!

It got away from me somehow.

My ball was in a ball game now.

It hit the man who sold the pop!

It went right on! It would not stop.

It went right for the man at bat.

I called, "Oh! no, do not hit that!"

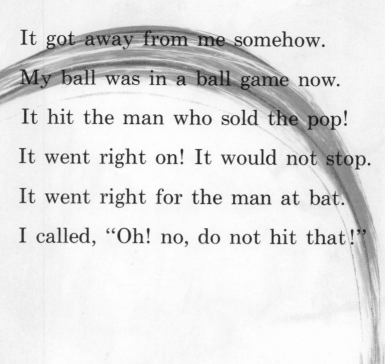

I saw a fat man in the band.

He had a fat horn in his hand.

Oh, what a thing to get into!

If it went there,

What could I do?

Oh, what bad luck!
My ball was stuck!

And so the fat man could not play,
For my red ball was in the way.
I saw him blow with all his might.
Oh, could he blow it out all right?

Oh, what a blow!

My ball shot out!

And it was gone,

Or just about.

I saw my ball head for a gun.

And then—oh, boy!—how I did run!

My ball came down, just like a shot.

What did it do?

Why, you know what!

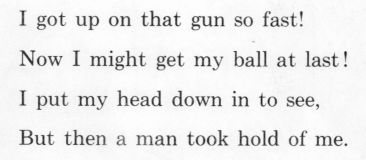

I got up on that gun so fast!

Now I might get my ball at last!

I put my head down in to see,

But then a man took hold of me.

He took me down.

"Get back!" he said.

"That gun

Could blow away your head!"

Then BOOM!

BOOM! BOOM!

Oh, what a thump!

I saw the gun

Just kind of jump.

It shot my ball

Up in the air.

How high would it go now?

And where?

My ball went high up past the band,

The tree, the game, the fire, the sand,

The box, the blocks, then past the man

Down in the hole.

I ran and ran!

My ball went over all the town!

And do you know where it came down?

My ball was home!

I ran so fast!

Now I could have my ball at last!

And I could put it on the string!

I was so happy I could sing!

But by the time I got home, too,

Someone—

I do not know just who—

Had put my ball back on the string.

That was a kind of funny thing!

But I was happy anyway.

I had my ball

And I could play!

I hit my ball. I made it fly.

I hit my ball as it came by.

It went around and then came back.

I gave my ball another WHACK!

I hit it high.

I hit it low.

I saw the string let go,

And then

My ball was on its way again!

Could this go on all day and night?

It could, you know, and it just might!